HERO TIME
with FINN & JAKE

THE ULTIMATE GUIDE
TO BECOMING
A GENUINE LEGEND

Written by Brandon T. Snider
Illustrated by Zachary Sterling

TITAN BOOKS

London

An Insight Editions Book

Furniture
of
CONTENTS

THIS BOOK DESERVES MORE THAN JUST A TABLE OF CONTENTS. IT DESERVES AN ENTIRE FURNITURE OF CONTENTS! IT'S THAT GOOD.
—FINN

You know what this book and my favorite kind of couch have in common? They're both SECTIONAL.
—Jake

TO THE HEROIC PERSON WHO FINDS THIS BOOK:

YOU'RE IN LUCK! This is a book **for** heroes, **by** heroes, and **about** heroes. If you're not a hero (or at least trying to be one), you have to turn back now. Seriously. This is not a joke! If you're a demon or an evil monster, you can't read this, because then you'll know all of our secrets. **So many secrets.** This book is filled with all the secrets that heroes share when they aren't battling ugly slime creatures and traveling to alternate universes. This book also has a lot of hot tips on how to woo princesses. You won't believe what princesses are up to when no one's looking. They get **crayzay**.

So if you're a big blob from a blobby dimension that wants to blob all over the place and treat people like blobs, we (Finn & Jake) command you to stop reading immediately and return to your world. No evil allowed. None. Zero evil. Zilcho evilo. **Take. A. Hike.** But only if you're a real-time jingle blaster. Or . . . maybe we (Finn & Jake) know that you, an evil person, have our book, and we put a bunch of wrong stuff in here to throw you off our scent (which can

be stank sometimes). Maybe everything in here is wrong. Maybe we're tricking you. That's the thing about heroes—they'll do whatever it takes to save lives . . . even if it means fibbin' a little.

But if you're a real hero (and not some nasty piece of zazzle)—**listen up.** This book will help you. It'll make you maximize your hero-ness, using patented techniques designed to help develop you into the ultimate instrument of adventuring. That's a fancy way of saying "rules." That's right. Rules aren't just for fools anymore. In order to be a hero, you've got to be down to learn.

We (Finn & Jake) are going to tell you all about the nutball adventures that we've had and how they made us into who we are today. The hero life has ups and downs. You're gonna have good times and bad times. That's the way it is. And this book will help you figure out how to hold tight when things get rough. **Trust**. Every hero has a different story, and when you put all those stories together, things can get pretty bloobalooby.

You can also learn from your enemies, too. Oh! Time to get serious for all you posers out there. Heroes are **not** about the bread. They're about helping people and learning. So if you're reading this book in a park just so people will think you're a famous hero and give you all kinds of jewels and fortune—**Take. Another. Hike.** Heroism comes from a place deep down inside, somewhere near your boingloings. It makes you get up in the morning, and it tucks you in like a little baby at night. It taps you on the shoulder when you see someone in trouble and says "Um, are you gonna do something about that?" We

need more heroes, so you better get it together before this book explodes into a million fairies! Haha. Just kidding. But you never know.

And if you don't like this book, what do **you** know anyway? You found a book and didn't return it to its owner. That's not what a hero would do.

What else, what else . . . ? Oh! We (Finn & Jake) almost forgot to tell you that we (Finn & Jake) collected all the coolest stuff from across the Land of Ooo so that you could meet all the cool heroes we're pals with and see where we come from. Don't tell **anyone** that you saw this junk, you hear? People might not know we have it.

Whoever finds this book must always use its knowledge for good. Did we (Finn & Jake) already mention that? You must always act like a **hero**. Or else. I think we covered that, too.

Well, anyway, that's the introduction. Hope you liked it. Oh, and if you're still reading this and are an evil warlord who lives in an old cave—this book is cursed, and now so are you.

Bye!

—FINN & Jake

WAS THAT GOOD?

Yeah, man. It sounds really formal, like something you'd read on a stone tablet from the top of a mountain!

IF ANYONE EVER TRIES TO PUT A HEX ON THIS BOOK, IT WON'T WORK. I ALREADY HEXED IT . . . IN A GOOD WAY.

GETTING STARTED

Congratulations! You're now a full-fledged hero! Time to go pick up your badge and start helping Old Lady Princess cross the street.

Yeah, right! Did you think all it took to be a hero was reading a couple of pages in a book?! **HAHAHAHA.** What a rube. You've got a long way to go, kid. It takes a lot more than that to become an epic hero. You're gonna have to read the whole book, and even then, who knows if you'll be totally ready to enter the hero biz. It's pretty intense stuff. **Pay attention.** There's a lot of prep work that must be done. Some of it's mental, some of it's physical, and some of it's emotional.

Is that right? I can't remember. All my notes blew away in the wind, so I'm pretty much playin' this whole "advice" thing by ear. But don't worry, you'll be fine. Me and Jake got your back. By the end of this book, you'll be fully prepared to embark on the most heroic journey of your lifetime. Cuties from all kinds of dimensions will be knocking down your door once they hear about the amazing **[INSERT YOUR NAME HERE!]**

First, you've got to make sure you get your origin straight. Did you hatch from a big fat egg and decide to fight crime one morning? Was your grandpappy kidnapped by Why-Wolves, and you had to become an avenging crusader in order to save his life? (Why-Wolves aren't super dangerous; they just love to talk so much that it feels like being kidnapped.)

It's a lot to think about, I know. Maybe this book is part of your origin. Maybe this book came around and **changed your life**. It's an option. You'll figure out your origin when you're good and ready.

My notes blew away in the wind, too.
Why is the wind SO STRONG?!?

WHO WE ARE

Why should you listen to us? Why **wouldn't** you listen to us? Who are you, Dr. Wisebottom?! Me and Jake have been heroes for a really long time, so we've got a lot of really solid wisdom to lay down. We came, we saw, we adventured. And now it's time to pass on our incredible knowledge to you, dear reader. You should be thanking us. With ice cream. And burritos. But we can get into all of that later. In the meantime, get out a pen and some paper. We're going to be throwing a lot of information your way. So many tips for budding heroes who are about to embark on their own journeys of self-discovery. Like, **a lot**.

But we gotta get our notes back from the wind first. I know, I know, you need some more details about me and Jake before you trust us. I get it. So off the top of my head, here are a bunch of heroic things we've done that should set your pretty little mind at rest.

- TRAVELED ACROSS A BUNCH OF DIFFERENT DIMENSIONS
- CHASED THE LICH ALL OVER THE PLACE
- FORMED A BAND
- BATTLED BAD GUYS ON A DUNGEON TRAIN

- BEEN TO THE FIRE KINGDOM A BUNCH OF TIMES
- FOUGHT OFF AN INVASION OF CANDY ZOMBIES
- HAD SOME RAGIN' SLUMBER PARTIES
- BECAME REALLY GOOD AT CARD WARS
- HUNG OUT WITH WIZARDS
- HAD CRAZY DREAMS

- FIXED A TRUCK
- SWITCHED BODIES WITH OTHER PEOPLE
- FOUGHT GHOST WARRIORS
- BEEN ON A DUNGEON CRAWL

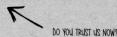

DO YOU TRUST US NOW?

A List of Stuff a Hero Should Have On Hand at All Times

- Eye patch
- Backpack filled with tools
- A viola
- Little people
- Fire guitars
- Robosuits
- An old porcelain lamb
- Swords! (We'll get into those shortly.)
- A stretchy best friend
- Spell books
- Your favorite stuffed animal
- A cosmic gauntlet (Any ol' cosmic gauntlet will do)
- Sandwiches

- A really good hat
- Feather capes
- The Armor of Zeldron
- A phone
- Warm sweaters

THIS IS A GOOD LIST, BUT, JAKE, WE REALLY NEED
TO REORGANIZE OUR NOTES BEFORE THE NEXT
CHAPTER. THE STAKES ARE TOO HIGH!

HOT TIPS

Here's some good advice to start us off on the right track!

1. Getting older is kind of cool even if you want to stay young forever.

• • •

2. If you show up at a mysterious castle for a masquerade party, chances are there's going to be a mystery involved. And if there isn't, then you should leave.

• • •

3. Starting a band with your friends can be hard, so make sure everyone is on the same page.

• • •

4. Princesses can be really moody, so tread carefully.

Okay, so we've learned a lot more than this, but if we told you everything now, then we'd have no book. A hero doesn't learn every single lesson at once. That would be insane! A hero becomes a hero because of the knowledge and experiences she (or he) accumulates during their lifetime of adventuring. Oh, wow. That was pretty good. I really know what I'm talkin' about. I'm totally not surprised though. I can be really enlightened when I put my mind to it.

Ugh, now we gotta go get our notes back from the wind so we can write the rest of the book. All our smart ideas are blowin' around the Land of Ooo for any ol' noob to grab 'em.

Oh! In the meantime, let's get started on a case. Good idea, Finn. Why thank you, Finn!

Dude, are you okay?

One quick way to get started on your hero's journey is to take on a mystery. There are always people who need help somewhere. Most of the time, no one knows what to do when stuff goes crazy. That's where you come in. Every time an injustice happens, someone complains to someone else about it, and then everyone has to do paperwork. So when you're looking around for problems to solve, all you gotta to do is spend hours reading all that paperwork to see which case is best suited to your particular skills. Sometimes stuff has a way of working out, so don't get stressed. Take on one mystery at a time, and you'll be golden.

Right now, Finn and
are really busy lookin
at our next big thing
So many to choose
from . . .

CASE #1
Authorities were called to a party in the Candy Kingdom where Punch Bowl was in attendance. He was seen being "loud" and "boisterous," according to sources, and was escorted home.

Where's the mystery?
The dude loves to party!
It's all good.

CASE #2

A group of Clown Nurses were seen making balloon animals and farting bubbles outside of the Tree Fort. They dispersed after a time and collectively rode away on a single unicycle.

NO MYSTERY THERE. CLOWN NURSES ARE FREAKY.
CASE CLOSED.

CASE #3

Gary the Mermaid Queen was seen poking her head out of the River of Junk. Bystanders were overheard saying, "That's not a mermaid! It's a skeleton lady!" Gary overheard these remarks, belched up a pile of sludge, and floated away.

Why do we get all the freaky cases?!

CASE #4

Gunter has been reported missing by the Ice King. He was last seen waddling around the castle. No other details are available at this time.

Gunter is so majestic. Like a king! But not, uh, an icy type of king. A penguin king, I guess. I wonder if he's a cuddler. I hope he is, the little cutie.

JAKE, THIS IS <u>THE ONE</u>. WE'RE HELPING OL' FROSTY BUTT FIND HIS PENGUIN!

STEEKERS

It's important for a hero to know how to fight! What I mean to say is that a hero needs to know how to defend herself (or himself). When some giant weenus tries to rob the Cosmic Bank, what are you going to do? Stand there and say, "Oh, please, Professor Weenus, don't do this! You're better than this! Blah blah blah!"? Yeah, that'll work. You're going to want to show that booger-eater your **hot fightin' moves**. Everybody knows about kicking and, of course, the classic "punch," but there are lots of moves that no one except me and Jake know about. Those are the moves that will help you defeat your enemies.

You might be asking yourself, "Finn, if nobody knows about 'em, then how do **you** know about 'em?" Well, reader, the truth is that I know a lot of stuff I don't tell anyone. Like how one time I heard Jake toot while he was sleeping. *So? Everybody does that.*

I even know about a place called the Fight-O-Sphere where . . . Well, that would be tellin', and I ain't tellin'! But I've been there a bunch of times when Jake was too busy sleepin' and tootin'. Oh, and the Fight-O-Sphere is exactly what it sounds like. I took down some of the grossest, hairiest eyeballs ever when I was there. That's right when I laid out my sweetest moves. **Bang-a-lang! Shmowzow! Eat justice!** And now here, for the first time, I'm sharing my most effective fightin' moves with you. **Tell no one.**

Where was I during all of this?

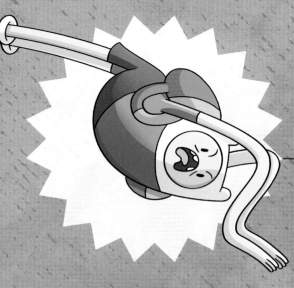

LIGHTNING BOLT *Strike*

Strike! Like lightning!
LIGHTNING BOLT STRIKE!!!

The SQUISH

Whenever you get yourself in a tight squeeze, **DO THE SQUISH.**

SHIMMY *Shammy*

Feel the power move through your shoulders. Yeah, like that. Shimmyshammyshimmy-shammyshimmyshammy.

Tooting SPIDER

Feel the toot move through you, then **RELEASE IT** like a spider!

COMBO *Move*

Only use the Combo Move if everything else fails! It's really serious. Here goes: Up, Down, Left, Left, Right, Right, Down, Spin, Down, Up, Left, Right, Left, Down, Spin, Up, Down, Jump!

I call this the Stretchypunch Scissor Spring MANIAC MOVE. It's kind of all over the place, but it gets the job done.

Welcome to the **Hall of Heroes**, where we salute our favorite courageous champions and daring defenders! Jake wanted to call it the **Palace of Coolios**, but we decided to go in a different direction. We wanted to have a special place where we could honor the heroes who have made a difference in our lives.

But sometimes people go overboard when they show appreciation for their heroes. They hug 'em and squeeze 'em and make statues out of 'em, and everyone comes to see 'em, and then people pay money, and it ends up being a big ol' crazy mess. That's not cool. We like celebrating the heroes in our lives, but we like being chill about it. Come on by, check it out, no presh.

And remember, that doesn't mean we don't think our heroes are stunning machines of honesty and truth that rock so hard they make a boulder look like a pebble! It means that their actions speak for themselves. We don't need to sell their heroism; their heroism sells itself.

Susan Strong

Our first inductee is . . . **Su-san Strong! Su-san Strong! Su-san Strong!** She's like a big muscly baby with the heart of a voyager who's also afraid of her shadow and doesn't know her own strength. Susan Strong is so pure of heart. That's what makes her a hero. She sees someone suffering, and even though she doesn't understand everything all the time, she knows she should help. She feels it in her guts. And she scratches herself like a dog. What I'm saying is that she totally knows right from wrong. She sees the big picture and lives by a simple code.

Oh! One time she danced with the Dancing Bug. I watched the whole time, and she was smiling so big. I think that might have been the first time she ever felt joy. But, then again, I've also seen her smile big while gnawing on a stick. She loves those things. What can I say? She's a lady of simple pleasures. I can relate—but not to the lady thing, just the simple pleasures thing.

Her pals in the Hyooman tribe were pretty weird, too, now that I think about it. I guess if I lived in an underground Beautopia, it might make me a little wonky as well. Don't they miss the sun?!

The Hyooman tribe seemed nice, and they really looked up to Susan as a leader, but those gills of theirs gave Jake the yeeshies. And let's get real for a minute—the Lub Glubs (Susan's sworn enemies) are pool toys that turn into terrifying creatures of darkness! Nope. Not into that. Too freaky. But to Susan? They're just some dummies that stand in the way of protecting her people. She's not afraid of them. She's not afraid of **anything**. Okay, she might be afraid of some stuff. I did see her freak out at her shadow once. I think she thought it was a ghost. But other than that, Susan Strong fears **nothing**.

Susan learned to communicate better because of Jake and me. We helped her loosen up and not feel so insecure about her talkin' skillz. It was hard for her to turn her thoughts into words. She really struggled with that. But then she fought through it like a beast and came out a winner! She's not an **actual** beast though. You know what I mean. And, in the end, Jake and I learned to communicate better because of her. It's the circle of . . . **communication**!

I didn't like it when Susan tried to drown me, but she said I had a hero's heart, so that makes up for it. She really helped me be braver.

There's a rumor that Susan became the new Cheryl (from Super Porp), but who knows? What I do know is that Susan Strong is an **unstoppable hero**. And, in the end, she always keeps it simple—be nice, or else!

Say how Susan didn't talk good.

JAKE, I THINK YOU MEAN, "WOULD YOU MIND MENTIONING HOW SUSAN COULDN'T SPEAK WELL?!!"

Yeah! That!

"Tough guy humans do not drink fake juice!"
—Susan Strong

SUSAN STRONG: THE SONG

SUSAN STRONG,
  THIS IS WHERE YOU BELONG.
HANGIN' WITH ME
  ON A FALLEN TREE.
DON'T YOU THINK YOU DESERVE THIS?
TO LIVE UP HERE ON THE SURFACE?
I THINK YOU DO,
AND I THINK ALL YOUR FRIENDS DO, TOO!

HOW LONG HAVE YOU LIVED
  IN THE DARKNESS?
I JUST WANT TO SHOW YOU THE LIGHT!
  BECAUSE YOU'RE A HUMAN,
  JUST LIKE ME, SUSAN,
AND I WANT YOU IN MY LIFE.
  SUSAN STRONG,
YOU TURN MY HEART ON.

19

Billy

Our next hero in the Hall of Heroes is . . . **Billy!!!** He's truly **the best**. I'll never forget the day Jake and I met him. It's probably my favorite day. *Really? But we've had so many favorite days.*

Billy is pretty much the ultimate hero. We might not have met him if it wasn't for Jake's nose. It's a good nose, a strong nose. **A schweet schnozz.** He uses it for all the regular nose stuff like smelling butts and whatever. It's that nose that led us right to Billy's sword. You know why? That sword stank! But a good kinda stank. Because it's seen so many battles and slayed a lot of stuff. There are so many different types of stanks that it's hard to keep them all straight. But Billy's sword definitely had the good stank on it. He calls it "Nothung." We used it to open up Billy's legendary Crack. Thinking about it still gives me the chills. It was that good. And then we met Billy himself. I was so starstruck! I don't even remember what I said.

That's right! Thanks, Jake. I asked him if we could be hero apprentices. Billy saw so much cool stuff in his life and fought so many battles. It's pretty amazing. I thought we could learn a thing or two from him since he's so humble and wise. What we learned from Billy is that even though he'd lived **so much life**, he never stopped learning. He never stopped growing. That's what made him a hero. Growing gets harder when you get older because you get stuck in your ways. Billy didn't see it like that. He got sick of violence.

Sometimes I get fed up with violence, just like he did. I wish I didn't have to use my fists and feet to stop every bad guy that comes along, but sometimes I have to. Especially when those bad guys are beating up on little guys. And I always protect the little guys.

Look, I really love beating up evil, but Billy helped me learn to suppress my warrior instincts and focus on helping rather than fighting. Don't get me wrong, I still fight. I'm a justice machine. But I'm always down to mix things up peacefully. Billy showed me that it can be cool to change for the better. Don't be afraid to grow, even if it means giving up something you like. That thing you like might not be the best thing for you. It might be tough, but you gotta do it. I might give up fighting one day. Who knows? I've got time to sort it all out.

You asked him if we could be hero apprentices.

BILLY'S SONG

Who's the greatest
warrior ever?
A hero of renown!
Who slayed an
Evil Ocean?
Who cast the
Lich King down?
Billy!

And that time the
evil Fire Count
Captured a damsel fair.
Who saved her
with such bravery
She offered him
her hair?
Billy!
Also . . . He fought a bear!
Billy!

I really hate The Lich for taking over Billy's body and killing him. It's really unfair. Billy was just like us. He even had a dog once! And he had this sweet girl friend named Canyon. Jake really wanted her to scratch his belly.

I'm glad we got to complete Billy's bucket list for him. I even overcame my fear of the ocean. His spirit helped me do that. Billy's spirit also told me that my real dad was alive somewhere, but I don't really feel like getting into that right now. I really miss Billy. He was my hero.

"Help people by being active in your community."
—Billy

Peeeeeeeeeebs

Princess Bubblegum is a super cool scientist who also happens to be the ruler of the Candy Kingdom. Oh, and just so everything's on the table: We have history together. It's totally not a big deal, but don't worry, I kept it really professional. That's something heroes do, too.

Princess Bubblegum is really incredible. (But don't worry, she's super chill about how incredible she is.) I thought it would be a good idea to get her perspective on being a hero since she's such an amazing smarty-pants.

Q&A: Princess Bubblegum

Q: Welcome, hero. Thank you for participating. Would you mind giving our readers your name, age, and occupation?

A: Okay. My name is Princess Bonnibel Bubblegum. I consider myself a scientist and seeker of truth. I'm also the ruling monarch of the Candy Kingdom, where I oversee an abundance of important matters. Thank you for inviting me to be a part of your book, Finn. It was very sweet of you to ask.

Q: Let's stick to the topic at hand, please, Miss Bubblegum.

A: You don't need to call me Miss Bubblegum. It sounds so strange and formal. Using my title, Princess Bubblegum, is fine. Or what about P-Bubs? It IS your nickname for me. . . .

Q: Ahem. I have noted your request, Miss . . . er . . . Princess Bubblegum. My first question is: What are some of the qualities you have that might be considered heroic?

A: Well, this is quite a first question. I understand that you believe me and my actions to be heroic in nature, and perhaps they are, but it's important to understand that they aren't exclusive to me. Anyone can be a hero. It takes hard work and determination, but it's achievable.

Having said that, I think there are a multitude of qualities one can develop in order to foster a heroic stature. For instance, be a good listener. There are many people in the Candy Kingdom and, sometimes, they have very different wishes and desires. As their ruler, I always listen to what they have to say. Everyone has different experiences that shape who they become. I always try to take that into account and put myself in their shoes. That way I can address their concerns respectfully and with a level of understanding.

As a lover of science, I also believe it's a hero's job to help innovate and improve the world around them. I strive to create useful tools that will benefit the greater good and help build a better world. Growing and changing for the better can be scary, but it's what people have to do in order to survive. We can achieve so many wonderful things through experimentation. Things that can help people in simple ways, like a robot arm that can assist a short person in reaching a high shelf! Or things that can benefit people on a wider scale, like a machine that makes sandwiches to feed the hungry! Not everything that gets created through innovation will be so useful, but that doesn't mean we stop trying to invent.

And, most important, a hero must acknowledge that we're all in this together in order to move forward. A hero shouldn't live apart from the people she (or he) serves. It might be commonplace to put someone with heroic ideals on a pedestal, but what if everyone possessed those qualities? What if everyone was considered a hero? That question always puts things in perspective for me. We must all strive for excellence, no matter our station in life, be it large or small. We must all rise up and be who we were meant to be. We can all be heroes—we just have to try our best!

Q: Wow. Um. Thank you for that answer. It's really good.
A: I'm happy to elaborate if you'd like.

Q: That's okay; I'll go to the next question: You're so busy inventing things and ruling the Candy Kingdom. Where do you find time for romance? WHOA. Sorry! I forgot to delete that one.
A: It's alright. I'll answer it anyway! Yes, I'm quite committed to my royal duties as well as to the pursuit of scientific innovation. However, I'm always open to new opportunities regarding affairs of the heart. Make sure you write that down.

Q: Noted. Next question: People have called you "sweet, kind, understanding, respectful, mysterious, super intelligent, cute, brave, and magical." How does that make you feel?

A: Oh my. Who said these courteous things? I'm very flattered to be considered as such, but so many compliments make me feel a little uncomfortable. I want to be very clear to your readers that I don't do the things that I do in order to receive praise. Of course, receiving praise can be a byproduct of positive actions, but it's not the end result I count on or expect. What's important is the work itself. When you put good works first, the reward will be in seeing the positive effects they have. Accolades will then become icing on the cake. (Note to self: Create a self-icing cake.) But it's very nice that you, er, I mean, people, think so highly of me. It makes me smile.

Q: What's it like being a scientist?

A: That's a rather simple question, isn't it? In short, being a scientist is amazing! The joy of discovery is an incredible feeling. I hold myself to a high standard, but I understand that creation is a fluid process wrought with highs and lows. I must always remember that patience is a virtue. Oh! That's something a hero should have—patience! Is there anything else you'd like to know? This interview is starting to become very fun.

Q: Cool! I mean . . . That's good. What do you think a common misconception is about heroes?

A: Hmmm. I understand what you're asking, but I struggle to reconcile your notion that a hero is so separate from everyone else. As I stated, we can all achieve greatness if we put our minds to it. Having said that, there are misconceptions that could benefit from deconstruction.

For instance, heroes get angry, too. They are not above having irrational emotional responses. That is a natural thing, though it helps when one learns from such reactions, leading to high levels of personal growth. I've been known to struggle with such dilemmas from time to time. I do not like idle gossip or foolish behavior. It makes me very mad. I try my best to understand the way I feel and then communicate those feelings to the people who need to hear them. And sometimes I need to scream.

Q: What's a crazy secret that you've never told anyone? It can be about you or someone else. GO!

A: Oh my. That's quite a question. I wasn't prepared for such an inquiry. But the thought of sharing a private anecdote is titillating, I'll admit. Confessions! Revelations! Should I also select something that has value as a heroic lesson? Oh, who cares! Let's talk SECRETS!

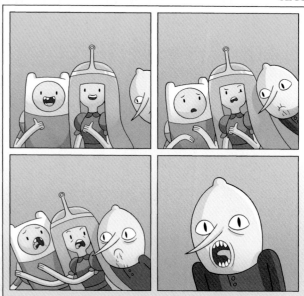

It's about Lemongrab! Okay. One time I poured all my leftover potions into a big pot and let it simmer for about a week. I was trying to make . . . well . . . that's actually a secret I can't reveal today. Sorry! I don't like to comment on experiments that are still in various stages of testing. Anyway, I closed off the area around the potion pot so that no one could tamper with it.

However, the scent was so alluring that it attracted the Earl of Lemongrab. He came bounding out of nowhere, broke through my defenses, and ran straight for the potion pot! I'd never seen such a thing. He was insane! I believe it has something to do with the familial relationship he feels with my experiments, but the proof is inconclusive.

There's still testing to be done. Feel free to contact me in five years when I've completed my study to the fullest extent.

So! Lemongrab takes off his clothing and jumps into the potion pot, lapping up gulps of potion, and then jumps out suddenly and runs away. He was gone for a full day before the Banana Guards spotted him sitting in a tree. Still nude, mind you. He wasn't quite sure how he got there or what had happened to him. The last thing he remembered was smelling "a thousand sweet souls," which makes sense in a strange way. The potion pot had an aphrodisiacal reaction when ingested but because of Lemongrab's physiology . . . well . . . It's quite complicated. But I never told anyone that story! Not because Lemongrab would be embarrassed, but I just don't have the inconclusive data yet. Oh my! I just remembered another secret!

Q: Princess Bubblegum, maybe it's time to move on?
A: Oh no! Are you sure? Let me tell you this one final secret. It's very good. One night, while I was going over some calculations regarding a particularly difficult experiment, I realized that I'd added incorrectly and botched the entire thing! My calculations were so off that I had to end the entire study and begin again. HAHAHA! I've never told anyone that before! It wouldn't be prudent to reveal which experiment this concerns, but what a doozy, am I right?!

Q: That's a doozy, for sure. And now it's time for our final question.
A: Oh? But I'm feeling so alive! I could do this forever! I'm discovering all kinds of things about myself! I feel so inspired to share myself with so many. . . .

Q: Sorry, Princess. We've got a lot of ground to cover in this book. Can't spare the space. Anyway, do you have any final advice for someone who wants to become a hero?
A: Oh. I see. Well, I appreciate the platform, Finn. I'm honored that you would allow me to be a part of such a wonderful project. My advice for anyone who hopes to achieve peace and prosperity in their lives is to give as much of themselves as they can to the world around them. Be kind to people. Fight to understand things. Learn!

And, of course, one must always take time to be with themselves. My alone time is crucial to my being able to serve my people effectively. But being a part of the world at large is also very important. A scientist should observe, but a hero must get involved. Dedicate yourself to world, and it will pay you wonderful dividends!

Q: Thank you very much for your time, Princess Bubblegum. I think you're awesome. I mean, our readers think you're awesome. Or they will. Um. You can go now.
A: Thank you, Finn. I appreciate your candor and kindness.

TO PB—

THANK YOU FOR LETTING ME INTERVIEW YOU. IT WAS REALLY NICE.

WE SHOULD HANG OUT SOMETIME OUTSIDE OF WORK OR SOMETHING.

AN ADVENTURE A DAY

A lot of people ask us, "Hey, Finn and Jake! How do you decide what amazing quest to go on each day? Do you wake up and meditate on it? Also, you guys are pretty spectacular." But choosing the right adventure isn't something we do lightly. It's not like we have a dartboard with missions on it and just throw darts till we hit a good one. That would be pretty lame.

We use a very sophisticated system of selection that takes into account all of the incredible possibilities that the universe has to offer. Hahaha. Just kidding. We use a calendar! All the best heroes have one. Not that we use it every single day. That would get boring. Or sometimes we're already in the middle of an adventure, so we don't actually need it. But it's there for us when we get stumped.

DAY 1

Seek out a bullying grass ogre and teach him a lesson he'll never forget!

DAY 2

Switch bodies with your best friend and do a bunch of crazy stuff while you're in it. But nothing mean. Only funny stuff, like pranks.

DAY 3

Commit a cosmic crime so you can break into the multiverse and visit your estranged father in prison.

DAY 4

SMILE.

DAY 5

Track a Crabbit Familiar to see what kinds of nasty things it does. Keep your eyes peeled for Sky Witches.

DAY 6

Take all your gold, and go on a wild spending spree!

DAY 7

NAP!!!

DAY 8

The mudscamps are under attack! Create a suit of armor for Woobeewoo so he can defend their freedom. It's what a friend would do.

DAY 9

Clean your Tree Fort. That thing

can

get

dirrrty.

DAY 10

Trick a magician into thinking that her wand is an all-powerful totem that can unleash darkness across the Land of Ooo. (But really it's a tree branch.)

DAY 11

HUMP DAY!

(Put a hump on your back and pretend you're an old crone.)

DAY 12

Throw a surprise birthday party for someone even though it isn't their birthday!

DAY 13

Smell the wind. Do you smell ghosts? Ghosts are every-where. Write down each scent you smell and see if you can figure out what kind of ghosts are around you.

DAY 14

HERO WORKOUT

DAY 15

Ask a wizard to remove one curse. It can be any curse, but they have to get rid of it. Cursing people isn't cool or fun. Unless the cursed person is an evil overlord. THOSE STINK.

DAY 16

Make sure your clothes aren't haunted by evil spirits. If they are, you'll need to transport yourself to the Spirit World. There you'll learn how to properly dispose of specters while maintaining the elasticity of your trousers.

DAY 17

Remember how awesome Billy was, and honor him by being totally peaceful and not fighting anyone, even though you want to very badly.

DAY 18

It's storming swords, so you can hang out at home and draw a story all over your walls. Make sure it's good and takes the reader on a journey.

DAY 19

Create a new identity for yourself. You could be a wizard baby, a Lub Glub looking for love, or a two-headed princess who doesn't have time for foolish nonsense.

DAY 20

Use your negotiation skills to make peace between Pagelings and Moldos, and end the secret Library War.

DAY 21

Find a desperate princess who yearns to be loved and show her a good time.

DAY 22

Follow the Ice King for a day. See where he goes. See what he does. **Take pictures.**

DAY 23

Grab a few
Hot Dog Knights
and stage
a fierce battle!
But just for fun.
No death.

DAY 24

Wash your swords.
(They stank!)

DAY 25

WILD CARD!

(Do whatever
you want;
the day is yours
for the taking!)

DAY 26

Tell Peppermint Butler
he's going to be the
new King of Freshness
and teach him how
to rule a kingdom. It
seems pretty easy, but
it's really not.

DAY 27

Use the
Sassage Flare gun.

Just once.

And then put it away.

DAY 28

SKIP DAY!
(This day is reserved
for skipping.
Only skipping.
No walking.
No sauntering.
No shimmying.
Skipping only!)

DAY 29

Check yourself for tiny
cat assassins that are
hiding in your nose.
Check your friends'
noses, too.

IF YOU SEE ME-MOW,
FIGHT HER!

DAY 30

Venture into the Astral
Plane and spend a day
in deep reflection. A
hero should always be
mindful of the past,
present, and future.

DAY 31

- Make an
  Everything Burrito.

- Share it with
  a friend.

- Wait for something
  awesome to happen.

JAKE'S LIFE

"I've lived a pretty great life. It hasn't been easy though. It never really is for a true hero." —Jake the Dog

You might think you know everything about your best friend, but the truth is that you don't. No one knows everything about anyone. But one thing I know for sure is that my best friend (and brother) Jake is pretty freak-a-liciously rad. Get ready for a major dose of hero talk with my number-one stretchy dude. Ladies, gentlemen, Candy People, I bring you . . . Jake the Dog!

Q: What is it like being a hero?
A: It's awesome.

Q: And what else, Jake?
A: Oh, um, well, it's really important, too. You want me to get real here, huh? I'm not too good at this. It's kinda hard, but I'll try. Actually, that's what being a hero is all about. It's about trying your hardest even though it's going to be hard. Maybe I'm not so bad at this gettin' real stuff.

So, yeah, heroism isn't always gumdrops and tight hugs, if you know what I mean. Heroes have to be brave and stand up for the little folks that people try to hurt. When you do stuff like that, it makes bad guys pretty mad. Heroes make enemies, that's what happens, but I got a theory. The way I see it? Bad guys are just good guys who grew in the wrong direction because they never had a hero to look up to. That's why I try to do stuff that inspires my kids to be better. I wouldn't be who I am today if it weren't for my family. They're the best.

Q: What does family mean to you?
A: A family is a bunch of people who support you during the good times **and** the bad times. Trust me, there'll be lots of both of those kinds of times. Even the most awesome hero can have a bad day. Just ask Billy. Oh, I guess you can't really ask Billy since he's dead. Anyway, family can be your mom, your dad, or your brothers and sisters. But the coolest thing is that family doesn't have to be **just** the people who you're related to by blood. Your friends can also be your family. It's whoever you're really close to and share secrets with and stay up late playing games with and stuff like that.

Q: Does your family inspire you to be a better hero?
A: Totally. They really keep me on my toes, especially my pups. Well, they're not really pups anymore, but you know what I'm sayin'. They make me want to be a good dad. Like sometimes if I get really mad, I'll want to freak out, but then I stop myself and think, "The kids are watching, Jake. You better get it together." I want to show them that heroes can make mistakes sometimes, too, but the important part is to learn from them. They challenge me, I guess. And I want to be able to show them how to be the best they can possibly be.

Charlie, Jake Jr., T.V., Viola, and Kim Kil Whan are all really different, which is great, because life is never boring. Even though they sometimes think of me as their dumb ol' dad, I know they get what I'm trying to do. We learn from each other. Is this getting too sappy? I feel like it's getting sappy. . . .

Q: It's fine. How do you feel about adventuring all the time?

A: I love it! I get to see so much cool stuff, like the Goblin Kingdom with all those little Goblins running around. I met Susan Strong. I've eaten the finest ice creams in the universe. Adventuring is pretty sweet.

Do you want me to get real again? Because I'm having some **real** feelings. The truth is that sometimes I miss my girl, Lady Rainicorn. Yeah, yeah, yeah. People want heroes to be loners who play by their own rules and throw caution to the wind, but Lady Raincorn's love fuels my heroic fire! I can't wait to come back home from a long day of questing and get all wrapped up in her warm rainbow body. She might have tiny arms, but they're really good at hugging.

Q: How does your family feel about you adventuring all the time?

A: I think they're cool with it. I think they're proud of me. I hope they are. And Lady knows what's up. She's Princess Bubblegum's bodyguard, for crying out loud. She's seen as much wacky stuff as I have.

And don't worry, even though we've got very full schedules, we always find time to be lovey-dovey.

Q: Who are your personal heroes?

A: I've met princesses and weird guys who live on the edge of the universe and control people's minds. But like I said, my family is pretty heroic (to me). I think BMO is cool for looking at the world in a weird way. Is that heroic? I think it can be. BMO also tries really hard. That's good.

Hey! I've got a good one! You know who my personal hero is? It's **you**, Finn. Because no matter what happens, I know you got my back. You're my brother-in-arms and my brother-brother. I'm getting misty over here thinking about how much you mean to me. Keep it together, Jake!

Q: Thanks, dude! But let's stay sharp till this interview is over. Do you have any final advice to offer someone who might be looking to get into the business of heroism?

A: Like I said, it's tough out there. Find yourself a good family. Always do your best. And don't be afraid to kick butt.

To my dearest Jake,

Thank you for dinner last night. It was extremely chewy and smelled a little bit like stanky socks, but that doesn't matter, because it came from your heart. We have so much fun together! Let's go to a movie next time. Maybe I'll let you snuggle up to me . . . then we can have some real fun. I'm so bad! You can't let anyone read this! Well, I've got to get going. I can hear Princess Bubblegum in the other room. She's upset about something. Poor girl. Bye for now. . . .

—Lady Rainicorn

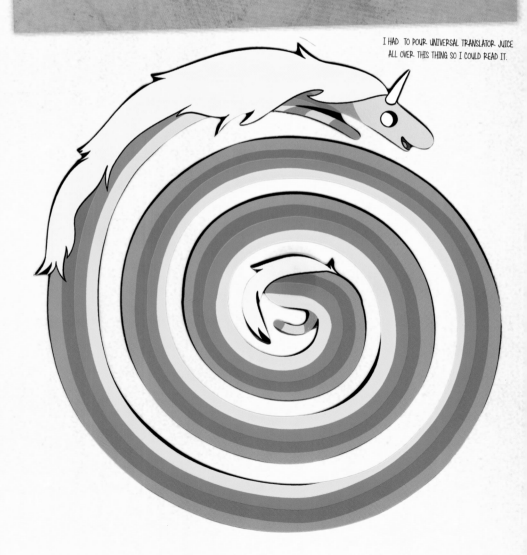

I HAD TO POUR UNIVERSAL TRANSLATOR JUICE ALL OVER THIS THING SO I COULD READ IT.

JAKE'S TO-DO LIST

DONE!

Spend some time with T.V. and maybe play a video game or two with him? Maybe we can go outside and play some ball, but he hates weather. ☐

Pick up a new pair of pixie pants. ☐

Figure out which ice cream is the best. ☐

Watch Charlie fly. She's so good. ☐

Let out that fart I've been holding. ☐

Take Viola to dinner for her birthday! ☐

Go to the dentist. ☐

Write a poem for Lady just because. ☐

Respond to Kim Kil Whan's letter about how I need to "take responsibility for my actions" and "stop wasting time" with "nonsense." Maybe he'll let me see Bronwyn? ☐

Bathe (in two months). ☐

Tree Trunks!

True love can inspire a hero to do great things . . . like bake apple pies! Baking apple pies is one of the most heroic things you can ever do in your life. And when people get their first taste of a hero's sweet 'n' tasty pie, it'll make them want to do good things, too. Okay, maybe that's not entirely true, but I'm totally right about how love can inspire heroism. Love makes people feel good. It makes them feel supported. And when a hero feels loved and supported, it's like they're **invincible**. Take, for instance, the case of Tree Trunks and Mr. Pig. They're probably the most famous lovebirds around (hold the "birds"). Tree Trunks works all kinds of magic in her kitchen not just because she loves making apple pies (which she does) but because Mr. Pig is right there beside her, showing support for what she does. If she needs something, he's there to help her get it. If she has a tough day and doesn't know how she's going to get everything done in time, he's there to calm her nerves. Together they're a **power couple**. Sometimes a little too powerful. They make out **a lot**. It can get creepy. But, hey, love is creepy.

I feel bad for thinking that Tree Trunks was old and bonkers back in the day. When she tries to be sexy, it still makes me feel weird. But as long as she keeps making those delicious apple pies, she can do whatever she wants!

I'll admit it: I've got a soft spot for Tree Trunks. I've got a lot of soft spots, but one of them is just for her. She makes awesome pies, but she can also hold her own when it comes to fightin' and stuff. Remember when we went searching for the Crystal Gem Apple and fought that giant wall of flesh with eyes? (I wish we could have played on it longer. It was so soft and blubbery.) Tree Trunks marched through that dark forest and faced danger right in the face! What kind of little elephant DOES THAT? The heroic, pie-baking kind, ya heard! Ah, those were good times.

Dearest Tree Trunks,

I'm writing this note as I watch you create your wonderful confections. To see the joy that baking brings you warms my heart. As you know, my heart wasn't always this warm. I've fallen on hard times. I've done things I'm not proud of. But your love lifted me out of that dark place and into the sunlight, where our love now thrives. Without you, I would be a lost soul, drifting across the chasm of life, desperate for guidance. But no longer. Being with you makes my curly tail stand at attention. Your sweet kisses are my life force. I'm eternally grateful to have found an elephant who truly gets me. And now, dearest Tee Tee, let my love lift you to new heights of culinary stardom. The road may not always be easy, but we'll walk it together. You're MY hero, Tree Trunks. And I love you.

—Mr. Pig

Tree Trunks is super cute. I ain't ashamed to say it. She almost kissed me to death, and I kinda liked it. I'm really happy that she found love with Mr. Pig and everything but . . . I'm a teensy weensy bit jealous of him for having her all to himself. She's the sweetest. Don't get me wrong, I love my Lady Rainicorn! Ain't no way I'm giving up my lady love! But, you know, a dog can give an elephant a compliment every now and again, right? Besides, Tree Trunks and Mr. Pig kiss WAY too much, now that I think about it. But how could you NOT want to wrap yourself around her like a tortilla? Tree Trunks is adora-sistible.

She does have a lot of ex-husbands though. She's so complicated and passionate. Elephants need to sow their oats, I guess. The bottom line is, Tree Trunks tries h to be a good person and care for the people around her. And she's good at b

That makes her a hero in my book . . . which is THIS b

I promise that no flies have landed on my pies.
Every pie I make is 100% fly free. I hate those nasty little things, buzzin' around all the time. If a fly lands on one of my pies, I'll throw it out and start over. No one deserves a fly pie. I accept all forms of payment, but you can have a pie for free, I guess. If you don't have any money, I'll accept a nice hug. How about that? But don't get too sweet on me, y'hear? I'm taken. —Tree Trunks

35

WIZARD BATTLE

Wizards are magical. Duh. But they're also heroes! Even though a wizard could turn you into a one-eyed frogbeast. (That's not as heroic as it sounds.) It takes a lot of commitment to learn the ins and outs of wizarding. You don't just put on a cone hat, wave your wand around, and start wizarding all over the place. It takes practice and dedication. That means studying all kinds of good stuff and bad stuff and then figuring out what works best. That also means a lot of trial and error. Heroes go through that exact same process, too. Not every hero makes the right decision the first time around. Mistakes can happen. That's why it's important to learn from them. And when you do learn from them, there's something magical about it. And let's face it—wizards can be out-of-their-mind crazy sometimes. They run around casting spells on people. They turn stuff into **other** stuff. Once I saw a wizard turn cold water into hot water, and I never told a single soul. It was our little secret. But today, the truth comes out!

Not all wizards have everyone's best interests in mind, but a lot of them do. It's unfair to judge ALL wizards based on a handful of bonehead dummy wizards. You gotta give it up to them, though, man. I heard they have to read a ton of spell books and ancient tomes and stuff. I don't even know what a tome is, but I like it. And even when a wizard studies their butt off learning spells and stuff, it all comes down to that one moment, that magic moment, when everything goes their way.

I didn't know how crazy Wizard Battle was until we went undercover and infiltrated one as the unstoppable MAGIC FIST! That thing was a big crazy free-for-all. It looks so different when you watch from the stands. Up close, it's pretty wild. All those wizards skulkin' around in their robes with their wands out. Abracadaniel even turned Ice King's nunchucks into a butterfly!

In the end, Finn got a kiss from Princess Bubblegum even though he cheated. BUT HEROES SHOULDN'T CHEAT. Unless they have to in order to save the day. Or get a kiss from a princess. Those are good excuses to cheat. If we hadn't cheated, then Princess Bubblegum would have been forced to kiss some hairy eyeball, and she would have hated that. So I guess we saved her life that day. That makes US heroes!

So much power in one place can be scary and dangerous. But I think wizards are heroes, even though some of them are pretty donked up. Wizards can be A LOT of things . . . but NOT a lot of things, too. A wizard could never be a demon king or a vampire queen. Those are totally different. This is a lot to think about. I'm gonna need to ponder it for a while.

Being a wizard is like being a part of a top-secret society with its own rules and stuff that nobody knows about, except other wizards. They've got secret handshakes, secret hideouts, and other secret stuff that we don't know about because, well, they're wizards. And the stadium where they do all of their wizarding and stuff has the best hot dogs ever! There's nothing like kicking back and enjoying a plump dog with a good bro. Bro dogs are the best.

SEATS AVAILABLE   NO OUTSIDE HOT DOGS ALLOWED

Where's the Grand Master's cats? He's always got weird little cats around him. Shifty suckers. I don't like it.

BETTER QUESTION—WHERE'S THE GRAND MASTER'S PANTS?

CONTESTANTS WILL FIGHT EACH OTHER WITH SPELLS FROM THE EIGHT SCHOOLS OF MAGIC.

NO SCIENCE! NO WEAPONS!
TO ENTER WIZARD BATTLE, YOU MUST BE A WIZARD!

PROGRESS REPORT

When a mystery comes around, you have to dive right into it. Ask all the right questions. Leave no stone unturned. You gotta give a little to get a little. Hardline 'em! (Those are all phrases I read in a book. I'm not entirely sure they apply here, but they sound pretty intense, right?)

Jake and I have been working the Gunter Case, and it's a doozy. Mostly because we have to deal with the Ice King, and he can be a real pain in the hams. But since we're professional heroes who deal with ham pain all the time, it's no big whoop.

First, we collected clues regarding Gunter's disappearance. Newsflash: We didn't find any. But I swear we looked! Gunter doesn't seem to have a lot of stuff anyway. Once we realized there wasn't anything to track him with, we decided to grill Ice King with as many questions as possible. He could be a suspect, after all! Me and Jake have dealt with him about a gubillion times before. He's a real piece of **ice**. I feel for the guy, I do, but he's a mess. The good news for him is that we are detectives of the highest order. That means we do our job to the best of our abilities, even if our client is a donk.

That's the thing about heroism: Sometimes heroes have to **save** bad guys from danger. Yeah, I know. It's crazy. But you do it because it's the right thing to do. Say there's some son of a bleepblop out there who does naughty stuff all the time cuz that's how he was raised to be. No one taught him how to be good. And say this poo brain got himself into trouble and needed to be rescued. You might think, "I'm not saving that dude! He steals junk and treats people like garbage!" But that's the thing—he was taught to do that stuff. Should he know better? Maybe. But people deserve second chances, especially when they don't even get a first chance.

So, yeah we're helping Ice King cuz it's the right thing to do, and maybe after we find Gunter, Ice King will recognize what we did and do something nice for someone else. Or he'll just run around naked. You never know with that guy.

CASE FILES

POSSIBLE SUSPECTS

RICARDIO ICE KING GUNTER

MISSING!
LOST PENGUIN

Adorable penguin. Answers to the name of Gunter.
Gaze displays a hidden evil.
If found, return to the ICE KING!

1-800-save-gunter   1-800-save-gunter   1-800-save-gunter   1-800-save-gunter   1-800-save-gunter   1-800-save-gunter   1-800-save-gunter   1-800-save-gunter

penguin.
A: I ALREADY ANSWERED THIS.
HE WAS RIGHT NEXT TO ME
AND THEN HE DISAPPEARED.

in this case?
A: I'm lost without this little guy. LOST. You gotta help me. I'm at my wit's end over here and my wit isn't even that long to begin with! I know we've gotten off on the wrong foot before, but you two are my only hope here. I'll pay top dollar! (Unless I'm paying that already.)

SWORDS!

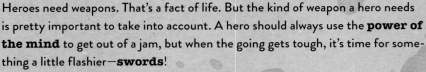

Heroes need weapons. That's a fact of life. But the kind of weapon a hero needs is pretty important to take into account. A hero should always use the **power of the mind** to get out of a jam, but when the going gets tough, it's time for something a little flashier—**swords**!

A sword is one of the most important things that a hero can own. It's not like some weirdo crossbow. Who shoots arrows anymore, right? Okay, probably a lot of people, but a sword is still crazy powerful and mega cool. And when you're not using it to battle the forces of evil, you can use it to butter your toast, and, um, you can hang stuff on it. If your sword is really shiny, you can look at your reflection and make faces. You should really get yourself one of these things. They're magical **and** "magical."

DEMON BLOOD SWORD
Okay, so Joshua is me and Jake's dad, and he created this crazy dungeon thing when we were babies. He thought I needed to be toughened up, which is crazy because I'm **already** super tough. So anyway, we had to go get this sword, but there was this nasty demon named Kee-Oth that used his own blood to make it, which is gross but also really cool. He's dead now. I actually broke the Demon Blood Sword awhile back and made a new one with frozen grape juice. Then I used it to trick Kee-Oth and defeat him forever! Just in case he shows up, all you really have to do is say "Kee Oth Rama Pancake" and **BOOM**! He disappears.

FINN SWORD
This little lady right here is super personal to me. "Little lady" is just a figure of speech. I mean, swords can be ladies, but ladies can't be swords. It's complicated. Anyway, FINN SWORD! In order to save my boy Prismo, I had to sacrifice a version of myself from another world. It involves a paradox. Which does NOT involve a pair of doctors, Jake. I know you were probably going to make a joke about that so I'm nipping it right in the bud. DON'T DO IT. So yeah, when I was messing with the time stream, some Finn from an alternate universe turned into this sword when his world got wiped out. It's freaky. At least he didn't die! Now I can use him any way I want. That doesn't sound right. . . .

ROOT SWORD
I found this one on a train when I was solving mysteries on my thirteenth birthday. Ah, those were the days. So young. So full of life.

It's pretty solid, cuz it's got a root handle. It's easy to grip like that. I like to strap it to my backpack when I'm out hunting monsters. Yeah, that's right, monsters, I'm hunting **you**! One time, I used it to take down this dumb monster that was shaking the Tree Fort. Don't mess with me.

SWORD OF THE DEAD

Whoa. It's been awhile, Sword of the Dead. You're looking creepy as usual. I got this guy from the Grasslands when Marceline's dad went crazy. I may have released him from the Nightosphere—and when I say "may," I mean, yeah, I totally did. They've got a lot of issues, Marceline and her dad. Anyway, I used the Sword of the Dead to slit this butt-thing in Hunson Abadeer's neck that had a bunch of souls in them. Gross, right?

PINK JEWEL SWORD

Hey! That's the sword that sliced my bed into pieces!!! **Not cool, Pink Jewel.**

GRASS SWORD

I bought this little number from the Grassy Wizard. That pudgy piece of grass put a curse on it. So . . . Grass Sword ended up becoming my arm. Yeah. I pretty much don't know if it'll ever take control of my whole body and cause even more trouble. DON'T LET THE GRASS CONTROL ME!

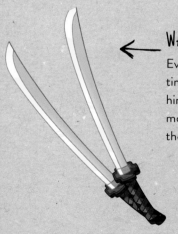

WAKIZASHI

Everyone knows that I've got a sweet way with the **laydees**, so one time I helped my slug buddy Snorlock find a girlfriend by showing him awesome sword tricks. And you know what **laydees** love the most? Awesome sword tricks. And guess what else? I don't really use these guys for fighting; they're more for show.

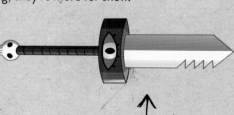

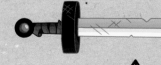

SCARLET

Aw yeah!!!! This right here is my girl! We've been through so much together. My golden sweetheart. I don't know where she is since she became four-dimensional, destroyed a black hole, and got lost in the Cotton Candy Forest.

JAKE'S SWORD

Hey! This isn't my sword; this is Jake's! He doesn't even know how to use this thing. It's so clunky and weird. How did this even get in here? SWORDS!!

PRINCESS YEARBOOK

Here we go! Now it's time for some heroic princess action. In the old days, princesses used to sit around and drink tea and gossip with other princesses about stuff like how long their nails are and how they love "the little people." Not anymore, my friends. Nowadays princesses are about **justice for all.** They rule. No, really, **they rule.** That's why they're princesses.

And watching over a kingdom is hard work. They make laws, and when people don't obey those laws, they kick their big butts all over the place. That ain't so easy because bad guys do whatever they want. But a good hero knows when to step in and say, "Clean up your act! The people aren't going to put up with your rule-breaking anymore!" That's the job of a princess.

And there's, like, a million of them. Finn and I found this yearbook thingie in the trash. Some princess probably got mad and threw it out the window or something. I feel a little weird reading these messages but not enough to stop. Sorry, ladies.

I DIDN'T EVEN KNOW THEY MADE A YEARBOOK.
IS THERE A PRINCESS SCHOOL I DIDN'T KNOW ABOUT?

I want to say thank you so much to all the amazing Princesses who devoted their time, energy, and royal stature in order to make this yearbook. What an honor it is to be surrounded by so many wonderful leaders!
—BREAKFAST PRINCESS

EGG-BREATH, I LOVE YOU!
—STRUDEL PRINCESS

Breakfast Princess

SUPERLATIVE: Crispiest Head Bacon
CLUBS: Princess Day Decorating Committee, Princess Day Organizing Committee, Princess Day Committee Committee, Band
QUOTE: "Okay, everyone, let's take a lunch break. And by 'lunch' I of course mean 'breakfast'!"

Muscle Princess

SUPERLATIVE: Most Likely to Not Be Able to Fit Through a Door
CLUB: Beauty Brigade
QUOTE: "My body needs JUICE!"

You are my sister in so many ways. I'm so lucky to have such a sweet sibling. Thank you for coming along with me on this journey and being there for me when things get rough. We laugh together, we cry together, and you always tell me when my bacon is too crispy. I'll always appreciate that. Sisters forever!
Love you.—BREAKFAST PRINCESS

EMBRYO PRINCESS IS SO REGAL. LOOK AT HER!

EP, I have yet to receive your registration dues. Can you please get in touch? Thanks!
—BREAKFAST PRINCESS

Embryo Princess

SUPERLATIVE: Best Amniotic Sac Overall
CLUB: Telekinetic Guild
QUOTE: ...

STRUDEL PRINCESS IS #1!!
—STRUDEL PRINCESS

Strudel Princess

SUPERLATIVE: Most Likely to Take Sides
CLUB: Pastry Pals
QUOTE: "Eat the berries, dip them in the syrup, whoop whoop, want me to show you how?"

Elbow Princess

SUPERLATIVE: One of Ice King's Most Precious Princesses
CLUB: Helping Hands
QUOTE: "I feel . . . incomplete . . ."

Gridface Princess

SUPERLATIVE: "I can create strong force fields. Is that superlative?"
CLUB: "Whatever you call that big group of whiny Princesses I'm involved with."
QUOTE: "Can I give you something later? I'm too busy inventing new modes of communication at the moment."

You didn't tell me you were going to use what I said!
—GRIDFACE PRINCESS

Blargetha

HEY! —Blargetha

SUPERLATIVE: Slime Princess's Sister
CLUB: Guillermo Appreciation Society
QUOTE: "I can't just pop out eggs on command. I'm an artisan."

He's real to me! —Blargetha

BLARGETHA—WELL, WHAT CAN I SAY? YOU'VE BEEN REALLY AWESOME TO ME DESPITE ALL THE DRAMA (YOU KNOW WHAT I'M TALKING ABOUT). PUT ALL OF THAT GUILLERMO BUSINESS BEHIND YOU. YOU ARE A STRONG PIECE OF SLIME, AND NO ONE CAN TAKE THAT FROM YOU! THANKS FOR TAKING CARE OF ME WHEN MY BERRIES FELL OFF. UGH. SO EMBARRASSING. IT HAPPENS WHEN I LEAST EXPECT. HAHA. YOU'RE THE BEST. LET'S HANG OUT SOON!
—WILDBERRY PRINCESS

LSP, I really love your style. It's so different! I know we only met once at a party, but I'd love to hang out sometime. Stay sweet and unique! —HOT DOG PRINCESS

Hey, Lumpy Space Princess, I just want to say that I know we don't always get along because you can be an insufferable glob, but I consider you one of my best friends, and I will always be there for you. Sisters till the end. —BREAKFAST PRINCESS

Those other princesses should be happy you even give them the time of day! You are SO OVER Brad that it's not even funny. Melissa can have him. Keep doing you, and stay away from drama bombs. Take it from me because I'm important. —DUCHESS GUMMYBUNS

LUMPY SPACE PRINCESS

SUPERLATIVE: Lumpiest
CLUB: Hot Boy-Watching Society
QUOTE: "You know, you guys can buy my book, *I Wrote A Book*, all over the place, right? I'm a famous author but very humble. WHATEVS, you don't know me. I do what I lumping want, when I lumping want to."

Daughter: We are very proud of you. Please come home and end your foolishness.
—LUMPY SPACE KING & QUEEN

Flame Princess

SUPERLATIVE: Warmest
CLUB: "Does my anger management support group count?"
QUOTE: "If you can't stand the heat, then WHY ARE YOU STANDING RIGHT NEXT TO ME?"

STRUDEL PRINCESS IS STILL #1!
—Strudel Princess

I DON'T GET WHY EVERYONE THINKS YOU'RE SUCH HOT STUFF.
—LSP

Hey, Phoebe! (Is it cool if I call you that? I feel like we're sisters.) I want to formally apologize about what happened on Princess Day. I had no idea that hothead was an offensive term, and I've taken steps to correct the matter. Emerald Princess should have known better than to use it, and I'm making her draft a VERY SERIOUS letter to you asking for forgiveness. As you know, I have many friends from the Fire Kingdom (Flambo is super cute!), so you know I'm on your side. Please don't burn me. (HAHA, I know you totally wouldn't, but you've just got to laugh, right?) Warmest regards! (That's not offensive, is it?)
—BREAKFAST PRINCESS

Wildberry Princess

SUPERLATIVE: Most Succulent
CLUB: The Produce-Ers   The Land of Ooo's #1 JAM BAND! — WP
QUOTE: "This is a medical condition, and I need a hospital."

I was just talking with Guillermo about you the other day—were your berries burning? Seriously, were they, because I know they bother you. Anyway, Big G (that's my nickname for Guillermo because we are in a relationship) and I agreed that you are really sweet for helping me stay strong. It's like everyone expects me to be perfect, but I'm just a piece of slime like anyone else. You GET that about me. Guillermo does, too (he says hi). I'm really busy with relationship stuff, but when G-Unit (we have a lot of nicknames) and I take some time apart, I'd love to see you! Stay fresh. —BLARGETHA

Skeleton Princess

SUPERLATIVE: Most Likely to Wear
a Skirt Made of Dead Birds
CLUBS: Bite Club, Skeleton Key Club
QUOTE: "CHOMP."

WHOA. That's one desperate wiener . . .

Hot Dog Princess

SUPERLATIVE: Plumpest
CLUB: Hot Dog Knights of the Roundtable
QUOTE: "A kiss from Finn would be a dream come true.
If anyone knows how I can make that happen, get in
touch! I'll pay top dollar!"

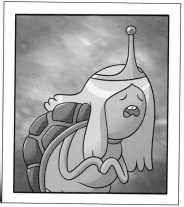

Turtle Princess

SUPERLATIVE: Most Likely to Revoke Your Library Card
CLUB: The Book Turtle Society (formerly the Book Worm
Guild, trademark pending)
QUOTE: "BE!!! QUIET!!!!!!!"

FINN & JAKE'S DREAM MENU

Every good hero dreams big. I'm not talkin' about boring old flying dreams, I'm talkin' about dreams that can change the world. Sometimes a hero might go to bed thinking, "Hey, how am I going to solve that problem?" and then they wake up and go, "Slamacow! I know how!" That's cuz they sorted everything out while they were in the dreamscape.

There are all kinds of different dreams that you don't need to fall asleep to have. For instance, making the world a better place is a good one. Free ice cream for everyone, all the time, for all eternity, is a very good one. But the bottom line is that dreams inspire heroes to do great things, even when those dreams are totally whacko.

Dreams can unlock a hero's imagination, and once that happens, it's on. Without an imagination, what good is anything? A great inventor like Princess Bubblegum might not have created all that stuff if it weren't for her imagination. I bet her dreams are real smarty-pants dreams with all kinds of smarty-pants stuff in 'em.

Dreams can help you work out problems and stuff even when they don't make any sense. One time I had a dream that I was being chased by Slime Princess because she wanted me to take a bath with her. I had to hide in a cave filled with nasty ol' cats. I was also dressed like a banana. Then, when I woke up, I remembered I had doctor's appointment! So, yeah, I think maybe that dream was trying to remind me of that. Or maybe I need to put a lock on my imagination after all?

Anyway, sometimes dreams are just plain fun. Sometimes they don't mean anything big at all. They're nuts. Me and Finn had a theory a while back that if you eat certain types of foods right before bed, they'll give you a certain type of dream. It sounds crazy, but we wrote down all of our findings and created a whole menu about it. The Dream Menu. Okay, now I'm hungry. I could really go for some ice cream right about now.

DAILY SPECIAL: THE PERFECT SANDWICH

Some sandwiches are created by magic and some are created by hard work. This one is created by Princess Bubblegum, so you know it's good. She uses a specific and precise process to create an enticing morsel of scrumptious sandwichery.

First, she builds the perfect tomato by fusing together a jellyfish and a red balloon. Then she karate chops it into three pieces, one of which is used on the sandwich. Next comes the lettuce—which is grown using special chemicals so that it's the exact size needed—which she shreds into perfect pieces by hitting it like a baseball. And the cheese is made by twirling a cow around a centrifuge to create a brick of cheese. Princess Bubblegum then molecularly unravels the brick into a perfect slice. All of these ingredients end up between two slices of bread. But these are not ordinary slices of bread. The magically fresh dough is sliced to perfection using laser beams refracted through crystals. Once all the ingredients are assembled, they're placed in an antigravity machine, where they come together to form **the Perfect Sandwich**.

PLEASE ALLOW FOURTEEN DAYS FOR ARRIVAL
DREAMS NOT INCLUDED

The Dream Menu

Welcome to Finn & Jake's Dream Menu, where each delicious bite invites you into the dreamscape with a welcome hand and a light slap on the tushy. Get ready for a dining experience you won't forget and might not remember. No sharing and no substitutions!

Appetizers

BABY HOT DOGS . . . . .

These tiny hot dogs are wrapped in baby blankets that keep them warm for your enjoyment. Make sure you sing them to sleep before you eat them. Then, once you enter the dreamscape, you'll be a fierce Hot Dog Knight who uses medieval weaponry to fend off attacks as you make your way through a dangerous labyrinth!

ANIMAL-SHAPED CHICKEN NUGGETS . . . . .

These fun-shaped chanticleer chunks come with peas, carrots, and mashed potatoes. Get ready to fight a megalomaniacal ice person with wonky emotions and paranoid tendencies who kidnaps people and does weird stuff in his castle. And that's just the first ten minutes of your nap!

CANDY SEEDS . . . . .

They're soft, squishy, and sweet. Pop one in, and you'll totally forget that there's a Seed-Wad growing inside you. Just kidding—that's only a dream. Or is it?!

SOFTY CHEESE . . . . .

Try a handful of gooey goodness, right from the can! It's not just a topping anymore—it's also a very poor hair gel. Polish off a couple cans, and you'll be visited by the ghost of Clarence, who'll deliver a dire warning: **Don't eat softy cheese, because you'll die!** Hmm. Maybe we should take this off the menu.

MACARONI SALAD . . . . .

Simple, classic, macaroni-covered—you'll be dreaming of grass-covered hills and picnics after a single bite. But be careful. Eat too much and you'll be visited by a team of Clown Nurses who are determined to find out what's wrong with you.
HINT: *You're filled with too much macaroni salad.*

FLAPJACK NOODLE STACK . . . . .

Hungry for a heaping plate of buttery noodles and pancakes? Well, here it is, partner. Once you've drifted off into sleepy-time, you'll have peaceful, reflective dreams. Until some dummy attacks you! Then it's time to put your ninja skills to use. Get ready to flap those jacks and kick some butt.

THE GREATEST SANDWICH EVER MADE . . . . .

Prepared with love, this sandwich has been called "most delicious" by Jake the Dog. It's sure to take you on a journey through time and space—and not just because of Prismo's world famous pickles. The meat has been prepared using a vacuum-sealed water bath of rosemary and thyme. Sliced cucumbers and Roma tomatoes adorn a pile of sweet yellow onions and diced boiled eggs to create a sharp taste sensation. A bird, some cream cheese, and a little bit of dill complete the sandwich, which is prepared on a toasted baguette. Additional ingredients include one lobster's soul, some salty tears, and, of course, bacon.

"What kind of dreams will I have once I eat this sandwich?" you ask. This sandwich is a dream unto itself and will not be questioned!

MEATLOAF . . . . .

This may seem like another simple meatloaf that's slathered in ketchup and filled with hope, but **be warned**. Once your head hits that pillow, you'll see how serious this meatloaf really is. Would some regular meatloaf shower you in a storm of swords? Would an ugly old meatloaf battle and then make peace with an ancient race of spider-ladies? The point is that you're getting a lot of bang for your buck with this thing. Put it to good use.

BATTLE ROYALE WITH CHEESE . . . . .

This meat castle is the last line of defense between you and hunger. It's two feet tall, speaks with an accent, and is accompanied by a bodyguard. Scarf it down and enter the **Dreamzone**, where you'll face off against the Grumblers, a race of gaseous toot-people who want to blow you away.

EVERYTHING BURRITO . . . . .

This thing has **everything**: eggs, cotton candy, a teacup, grapes, a waffle, a spatula, a glass of lemonade, a hot dog, a frying pan, a pineapple, spaghetti and meatballs, a milk carton, tacos, a carrot, a tomato, turkey, French fries, a banana, lettuce, bacon, grapefruit, strawberries, hamburgers, noodles, cheese, a speared olive, a ham, buttered flapjacks, a bowl of cereal, half an apple, a donut, sandwiches, some pretzels, a little poison, spam, two oranges, a plum, a loaf of bread, cake, chocolate cake, a pumpkin, pumpkin pie, beans, a tortilla, and a lemon wedge.

As for the type of dreams you'll have, well, that's the thing—**it's a secret.**

Beverages

HONEY ENERGY DRINK . . . . .

Honey is made from the freshest, sweetest, stickiest stuff around. You won't have **any** dreams after downing a barrel of honey because **you won't go to sleep**. You may even stay awake forever. Keep partying, and see what happens.

SUPER PORP . . . . .

What's in Super Porp?! You ask too many questions! It's a flavorful mystery. Cheryl knows, but she's not telling. Where is Cheryl, anyway? Just drink it and shut yer yap! Once you fall asleep, you'll dream of life underground, working in a Super Porp factory that's being guarded by a nasty dog. Fun!

BUG MILK . . . . .

Have you had a long day working as a clown at a Bug Circus? Drink your cares away with a nice fresh glass of Bug Milk. You won't dream about **anything** after you gulp down this creamy delight—instead, you'll physically travel to the Nightosphere, where you'll be confronted by the frightening Hunson Abadeer. Don't forget to bring a magical talisman. You'll need it.

Why not treat yourself to a refreshing libation? You TOTALLY deserve it!*

Desserts

SUGAR BOWL . . . . .

A delicious bowl of fresh sugar awaits you. Why not pour one down your throat? A few yawns later, and you'll be passed out fighting dirty cyborg fairies with laser arms. But what happens when a Swamp Giant arises from his watery grave? Go to bed and find out!

BMO CHIP ICE CREAM . . . . .

Crunchy microchips and a flaming strawberry puree perch atop a mound of scrambled egg–flavored ice cream. Two bites in and you'll be passed out in a digital world hidden deep within BMO's mind. Mathematical? Indeed.

FLAKIES! . . . . .

Flakies is really just a pear. One bite will have you thinking you're a Snow Golem who's eating a box of crispy bran flakes. But, really, you'll be asleep in a chair with a half-eaten pear.

You may not deserve anything. Eligibility to be determined by your own mind.

PRISMO

Perspective. Everyone's got one, amiright? Some folks lead really simple lives and that gives them a certain type of perspective on stuff. They see things differently than, say, an omnipotent wish master who can bend space and time. But that doesn't mean you treat any of 'em differently.

So if you're a hero, you need to learn as much as you can about **all** types of people so you can understand 'em better. A good hero takes a walk in other people's shoes in order to get perspective on things.

A good hero listens to people's concerns and learns about the stuff they're going through. A good hero finds out why people think the way they think. That's what gives them perspective!

Our pal Prismo knows all about perspective. He can see everything that's happening all the time because he's one of those omnipotent wish masters I was telling you about. He's got the best pickles and the best parties. He's so super chill. One time I puked in his hot tub from eating too many snacks. He even helped me and Finn change our own histories. Who does that? Prismo, that's who! He's a personal hero of mine because he saved my best buddy's life. That's Finn, by the way. When Finn wished that The Lich never existed, he accidentally messed up everything and ended up in some other dimension. But we got him back! Thanks to Prismo.

Prismo can really see things for what they are. He's a straight shooter, man. I like a hero who tells it like it is. I bet he gets pretty lonely in his timey cube box thing. Cosmic Owl stops by to hang and chill out sometimes, but I wonder if Prismo ever wishes he could play outside.

Aw man, this is making me hungry for pickles. Prismo's pickles make me wish I were eating pickles right now. Whenever I have one, it's like my stomach is filled with fighting butterflies of love. And his **parties**! Prismo throws the best parties. There's face painting and board games, and one time Peppermint Butler was breakdancing till the break of dawn. Good times, good times.

We've had a lot of deep talks, too. Prismo's parties are all about gettin' to know each other. We've shared stories about our adventures and discussed whether we made the right choices or not. It's important to do that stuff. No shame in sorting out the stuff that's in your brain. Every hero does it. Sometimes you need an outside eye (that's **not** an eye that's outside your body) to ask questions you might not have asked yourself. Prismo does that. He's the best. And to think—he's the dream of a wrinkly old man. The best wrinkly old man that ever was! So I guess what I'm saying is, you don't need to be some hard-partying, wish-granting, skinny, all-powerful pickle-maker to be a hero. You just need to keep things in perspective.

PRISMO'S PICKLES

HELLO, I'M PRISMO THE WISH MASTER. I EXIST IN THE PAST, PRESENT, AND FUTURE FROM HERE IN MY TIME ROOM. IT'S PRETTY NASTY. NASTY JAZZ! I ALSO MAKE PICKLES THAT FOLKS HAVE SAID ARE OUT OF THIS WORLD. BUT I'M NOT GOING TO LAY HERE ON THE EDGE OF THE UNIVERSE AND TELL YOU THAT MY PICKLES ARE THE BEST. TRY ONE FOR YOURSELF AND SEE. I'VE GOT YOU COVERED!

—PRISMO

ALIAS: JAKE THE DOG

Have you ever wanted to be someone else? **Join the club, bro**. (We meet at the Tree Fort.) But seriously, it's okay to want to be someone else sometimes. Lots of heroes have secret identities and aliases that they use to go undercover during their investigations. My pal Jake can be just about anybody. He is, what we call in the hero business, a master of disguise.

Jake's stretchy powers have seen a lot of action over the years. He's a very versatile hero, I'll have you know. And versatility is great because you can become anyone you want to be. That's a sweet skill to have for when you have to infiltrate evil empires. It's also good when you don't feel like being yourself. Not that you (or Jake) should have to be anyone but yourself, but it's nice to have options.

SIR JAKE: BARON OF THE GRASSLANDS

Sometimes I wonder what it would be like to be a real baron. All powerful and stuff, commanding armies and doing cool baron stuff.

RANDY BUTTERNUBS
That was a good top hat.

WIZARD JAKE

I don't know if I'm cut out to be a full-time wizard, but I do know that a guy in a wizard robe gets a lot of chicks.

BUTTERFLY JAKE

I made a pretty good butterfly, huh?

THE CONDUCTOR

You had a good time when I was a Candy Conductor and threw you that mystery train birthday, right, Finn? WE ALMOST DIED.

Is that a yes? OF COURSE IT IS.

GUT GRINDER

That was a weird one. I blame Sharon.

MARCELINE

Looks can be pretty deceiving. You might see Marceline as an ancient demonic force of evil just because she has black hair and is a Vampire Queen. But that's not really fair. She's so much more than that. She's an artist, a musician, a daughter, a friend, and a pretty sweet basketball player, too. But if you base your opinion of her on what she looks like, you would never know there's more to her than pale skin and long black hair.

Heroes come in all shapes and sizes. They can be big, small, lumptastic, or noodle-y. Get over it. Seriously. You don't have to have big, bulging muscles and flowy capes (even though the right cape can make anyone look super). You don't have to smile just because people think heroes should be happy, smiling little flowers all the time.

And another thing—yeah, Marceline's dad is Hunson Abadeer, Lord of Evil, Ruler of the Nightosphere, but that doesn't mean anyone should hold it against Marceline. Even if you've got a dastardly ol' papa with creepy vampire teeth who tries to eat people, you can still grow up to be a hero. Trust me.

Wow, I sound really defensive. I can be really protective of Marceline because she gets misunderstood a lot. It's not fair. Life's not fair, I know. But we gotta accept the complexity of life! Man, I'm emotional today. Here's Marceline!

Q: Marceline, did you just wake up?
A: Yeah. What is this for again?

Q: It's for a very important book about the trials and tribulations of being a hero. Me and Jake are writing it.
A: Oh. And you're interviewing me? Guess finding real heroes was tougher than you thought. You're really scraping the bottom of the barrel, Finn.

Q: Nope. You're considered a hero by our standards, and I don't scrape barrels. Never have, never will. Let's start the interview. Would you mind giving our readers your name, age, and occupation?
A: I'm Marceline. I play bass guitar and write songs. I'm only as old as I feel, and how I feel changes daily.

Q: What are some of the qualities that you might consider heroic?
A: Edge.

Q: Anything . . . else?
A: Is this a setup? Are you just looking for a headline? I'm not giving you some sugar-coated inspirational like a candy person. If you want me to tell you that heroes should save people and do everything the right way, that's a bunch of [CENSORED].

Q: Would you say that you're in a "mood" today?
A: Yes. I'm in a mood. Isn't everyone? I had to get up early to do this interview, and I haven't had anything to eat today. And you're asking me questions I'm not prepared to answer for a book I don't know much about. So, yes, I'm in a mood, and I don't know what you want me to say.

Q: Why don't you just tell me what you think?

A: Sigh. I can do that, I guess. [Pause] You want to know what makes a hero? Fearlessness. Nothing to be afraid of then; nothing can hurt you. Don't play it safe all the time. Take risks. You don't learn anything from staying home and eating a bunch of junk all day and night. Live your life. Make mistakes! If you're going to get hurt, you might as well get hurt when you're doing something you love or while you're experiencing something new. And have a sense of humor about the whole thing too. That doesn't mean you have to crack bad jokes all day. Just . . . I don't know . . . Don't be boring. Spice things up.

Q: How do you spice things up?

A: Pranks! But don't do really mean stuff. I prank you because it's easy, and you're cool. Don't prank people you hate; prank people you like.

Q: Can't that get you into trouble?

A: Yes. That's the point: Get into trouble! Trap yourself in a scenario you've never been in, and see how you get out of it. I'm a thousand years old, trust me. Things like that'll help you not get bored. It'll also distract you from doing vampire stuff, if you're a vampire. Heroes don't come in neat little boxes. They're messy and can be wrong sometimes. And you can't rely on a hero to save you. You can hope they do, but that doesn't mean they will. Here's a tip: Sometimes heroes let you down, so don't get

too attached. You can't rely on someone else to teach you lessons all the time. You have to just live your life and absorb the lessons as they come. The struggle is real.

Q: What are some struggles that you've faced?

A: Getting out of bed. Dealing with my family. Coming up with the perfect song. Listening.

Q: What are some of your extra-normal abilities?

A: Just your run of the mill necromancy. A good bit of shape-shifting. Some telekinesis, some pyrokinesis. I can turn invisible.

Q: How do you stay grounded?

A: Rise above it. Literally. I can levitate.

Q: Can you talk about your dad?

A: No.

Q: Can you talk about Hambo?

A: Sure. What do you want to know? Hambo was there for me when no one else was. He was my rock. He's also a stuffed animal. I don't care if people think that's weird. Hambo helped me through some tough times. He's kind of my hero. When things with my dad were really annoying, I could talk everything out with him. He was a good listener. It helps to have someone who'll listen to you, who'll help you work stuff out. Otherwise you're just talking to yourself. But that's okay, too.

Q: Is that what you do when you have a bad day? Talk to yourself?

A: Ha! No. Weird. Talking to yourself is fine for other people, but not me. And I'm not some "journal girl" either. I don't need to write notes to remind myself that I'm "worth it."

Q: Are you sure?

A: Yes. Why? What do you know?

Q: Nothing. What's a crazy secret that you've never told anyone? It can be about you or someone else. Go!
A: What?! Why would I tell you that?!

Q: Because other high-profile heroes have.
A: Oh. Like who?! I bet Princess Bubblegum did, didn't she? She probably loved being asked that question. She's so predictable.

Q: Well, then, we're at the end of our interview. But there's just one more question I'd like to ask. What if someone were to find a personal item that belonged to someone else? And let's say that the owner might not want other people to see this item. Would you return the item or use it as an instructional tool so that others may better understand the complexities of our unique and humble emotional existence?
A: . . . ZZZZZZZZZZZZZZZZZZ . . .

Q: And she's asleep. Thanks again, Marcy.
This is a note from Marceline to Marceline. It's pretty personal. This note is top secret. You cannot tell Marceline that we have this stuff and yes, I'm aware that fibbing is not heroic. We're making an exception in this case, and here's why. Everyone goes through dark times. Even the nicest little baby in the world has had a bad day where they don't just want to throw in the towel, they want to wrap themselves in it and teleport away. (Some towels can do that.)

OUR INTERVIEW WITH MARCELINE.

We always want to hide that dark stuff because we're afraid people will think differently of us if they find out. That's why we gotta share all of our experiences—the good, the bad and the . . . I forget the third one.

Marceline has darkness inside her. So do I. So does Jake. So does everyone. Don't pretend like you don't. But when the darkness gets to be too much, you gotta chase it down, hug the toots out of it, and show it that there's a better way. We try to do that with Marceline, even when she doesn't want to hear it. Me and Jake poured our souls out all over this book as if they were juicy sauces. So you know we're not full of poo or

something. We're sharing stuff we've never told anyone.

And maybe Marceline already knows we have this stuff anyway. We could be tricking you to find out if you're a tattletale. Maybe this is a test. Paranoid now, huh? You should be.

I feel weird about this stuff. I mean, I get that heroes can get depressed and whatever, but these notes are really personal and private. Also, I don't want to die! She's scary, dude. I get your point about darkness and how we all got a little rattlin' around in us, but she will straight up murder me! I'm not into that.

Hey, Marceline, it's me, Marceline. I'm writing this note to you before bed, and I want you to wake up tomorrow and read it. I know you've got a lot on your mind. I know things have been tough lately, but I need to remind you of a bunch of stuff. Remember all of this.

Here goes: You have awesome hair. You can play bass like a monster of rock. You love to sing. You've got a sweet vampire kick. You have a big heart, and it's okay when it gets hurt. Don't listen to what your enemies say about you. You are punk. Listen to your friends. Don't be afraid of getting hurt. You can levitate, turn invisible, raise the dead, and shape-shift. There are a lot of people who would die to do that stuff. (Hee!) You can slam dunk a basketball. You make music. You are a vampire. You are a demon. You are fearless. You are worth it. Today is a new day, and you're going to be fine.

—Marceline

PILLOW WORLD

Okay, readers, it's time to get **deep**. And a little freaky. A hero will go through a lot of adventures in life. Heroes see and do more than most people. After a while, it all runs together, but that's when you need to keep your eyes open the most. It's essential that a hero remembers to always, always, always be ready for the unexpected. Strange stuff happens, and you never know when it'll go down. Life will throw you curveballs, fast balls, and balls balls. You gotta know how to catch 'em.

This is going to sound super weird, but stay with me. One time, Jake and I were playing in a pillow fort. I was kinda upset at the time cuz Flame Princess didn't think I was as funny as I really am (her loss). I was in a funk and needed a little Finn Time, so I went deep into the fort and ended up in a totally different dimension made entirely of pillows. For real. I'm not making this up. Jake thinks it was a dream, but he also bites his own butt when it itches.

My memories are super crazy hazy, but I drew some pictures of the stuff that I remember. I met a girl named Roselinen and grew a beard! Oh, and me and Roselinen had kids (I was there for a really long time). Their names were Bonnie and . . . Jay, I think? Lots of other stuff happened, like when I fought the Blanket Dragon and visited the oracle Rasheeta, but that doesn't matter right now. What matters is that I got used to living in the Pillow World. It felt like what I needed to do at the time. I didn't just get wrapped up in the moment; I embraced the new experiences I was experiencing. I arrived when the people of Pillow World needed a hero, so I had to be that hero, even if it meant leaving everything I knew behind. Life threw me a curveball, and what could I do but catch it?

GO-GO BMO

And now one of the most important things you'll ever read in your entire life. It took a while, but we're finally here. Can you feel it? Are you tingly? Get tingly! But, seriously, this part is **slam bam in a can**. We're about to talk about one of the most important parts of the hero bidness—**sidekicking**.

Sometimes sidekicks can have a bad rap, but the sidekick I'm gonna tell you about today is a bad (meaning good) **rapper**! That sounded cooler in my brain than it looks on the page, but I'm keeping it here as a lesson. It's up to you to figure out what that lesson is, though, because I've got to move on. This book is running late.

Back to bidness! A good hero knows when she (or he) needs a little assistance—a helping hand, a trusty ear (or a ton of other cool body parts). That's where a sidekick comes in. They're one part friend with a dash of helper and a sprinkling of wise oracle. It's a big job. A sidekick has to support a hero while being a unique and gutsy creature in their own right. A sidekick isn't just for show. Sometimes they have to be better than the hero they support. They have to be one step ahead of the game in case their hero buddy ends up in trouble.

Who gets heroes out of jams? Sidekicks, that's who. Not always, though. Sometimes they're not cut out for action in the field, so they mostly stay back at the base and deal with all the other stuff that comes with being the pal of a thrill-seeking swashbuckler. But that's cool, too. No shame in the game.

Jake's Good Qualities for A Sidekick to Have:

- Trustworthiness
- The ability to play music
- Fun-ness
- The ability to play videos
- Hilariousness
- Sweet skateboarding skills
- The ability to play video games
- Doesn't object to tickling
- The ability to take pictures
- Must be an awesome chef
- A curious spirit
- A kind heart
- Can protect your Tree Fort if you get stuck in another dimension for an extended period of time

Me and Jake and have the best sidekick in all the multiverse. You might have heard. That's right: BMO has entered the Tree Fort!

BMO is pretty much the most incredible sidekick of all time. If Princess Bubblegum did a scientific study on sidekicks, she'd find out that BMO takes the cake. Actually, BMO doesn't just **take** the cake, **BMO gives it**! (I'm so tired.)

Do you like to watch videos? I bet you do.
Spin the Wheel of Heroic Deeds and watch
the memories inside my mind -BMO

WHAT HAVE WE LEARNED?

Here we are. The moment of truth. We threw a lot of stuff at you, dear reader, but the question remains: Did you catch it? It's okay if you're still processing everything. Take your time. It took me and Jake a day or so before we became the adventuring heroes you see before you, so we totally understand. In the meantime, you can go through this list as a reminder of all the butt-slamming truths we dropped on you.

★ HEROES NEED TO KNOW A LOT OF SWEET FIGHTIN' MOVES IN ORDER TO KICK MAXIMUM PATOOT. BUT YOU CAN ONLY USE YOUR FISTS AS A LAST RESORT. A PEACEFUL PATH CAN BE PRETTY COOL, TOO.

★ IT'S OKAY TO IDOLIZE YOUR HEROES AS LONG AS YOU REMEMBER THAT THEY'RE FLAWED JUST LIKE YOU AND EVERYONE ELSE.

★ PRINCESS BUBBLEGUM IS AMAZING.

★ CHOOSING THE RIGHT KIND OF ADVENTURE REQUIRES A VERY PRECISE AND SPECIFIC SELECTION PROCESS OF WHICH THERE ARE MANY VARIABLES. THAT'S WHY WE MADE A CALENDAR THAT TELLS US WHAT TO DO.

★ IF YOU'VE NEVER TASTED ONE OF TREE TRUNKS'S DELICIOUS APPLE PIES, YOU DON'T KNOW WHAT TRUE LOVE IS!

★ WIZARDS ARE REALLY GOOD AT BATTLING. SOME MIGHT SAY THEY'RE SO GOOD IT'S . . . <u>MAGICAL.</u>

★ EVERY HERO NEEDS A GOOD SWORD, EVEN IF IT'S JUST FOR SHOW. BUT IF YOU'VE GOT ONE, WHY WOULDN'T YOU USE IT TO SLAY PILLOW DRAGONS? IF THEY EXIST, THAT IS. YOU CAN ALSO USE SWORDS TO MAKE SHISH KABOBS. A GOOD SWORD IS A MAN'S BEST FRIEND!

★ PRINCESSES ARE REALLY GOOD AT ORGANIZATION. AND SOME OF THEM CAN BE A LITTLE INTENSE. (<u>GO STRUDEL PRINCESS!</u>)

★ DREAM BIG, AND MAKE SURE YOU ALWAYS EAT THE RIGHT THING BEFORE BED. FILLING UP ON ICE CREAM SOUNDS FUN, BUT IT CAN ALSO MAKE YOUR BELLY ACHE. OH, AND IT MIGHT CAUSE NIGHT POO.

★ A HERO SHOULD ALWAYS KNOW THE RIGHT THING TO SAY, EVEN IF IT'S IN A SECRET LANGUAGE THAT NO ONE ELSE KNOWS ABOUT.

★ IT'S EASY TO HAVE PERSPECTIVE WHEN YOU LIVE OUTSIDE OF TIME AND SPACE IN A CUBE WITH A HOT TUB. ALSO, PRISMO'S PICKLES ARE WHY HEROES DO WHAT THEY DO.

★ WHEN YOU'RE NOT SAVING LIVES AND SWINGIN' THAT SWORD, REMEMBER TO TAKE A LOAD OFF AND RELAX A LITTLE. HEROES GOTTA PARTY, TOO. IT'S ALL GOOD.

★ HEROES CAN HAVE AS MANY DISGUISES AS THEY WANT AS LONG AS THEY DON'T SECRETLY PRANK PEOPLE WITH THEM ALL THE TIME.

★ EVEN THE BEST AND MOST HEROIC PEOPLE HAVE A LITTLE BIT OF DARKNESS INSIDE OF THEM. IT HELPS TO WRITE SONGS ABOUT IT.

★ IF YOU EVER WAKE UP IN A WORLD FILLED WITH PILLOWS, JUST GO WITH IT.

★ BMO IS SOLID. LIKE, THE MOST SOLID EVER. SERIOUSLY. SO GOOD.

★ ICE KING IS BONKERS AND REALLY DIFFICULT TO DEAL WITH SOMETIMES. BUT WHEN HE NEEDS HELP, YOU GOTTA HELP HIM.

★ YOU COULDN'T ASK FOR A BETTER BEST FRIEND AND BROTHER THAN JAKE THE DOG.

So now it's your turn to go out into the world and be the best hero you can be. You're like a baby bird that me and Jake raised. Go and fly into the heavens!

But seriously, I hope this book helped you realize that being a hero isn't always easy. It takes a lot of hard work and understanding, but it's not impossible. And it's worth it in the end when you realize the difference you make by helping people. You could do something heroic just one time, but that might be all it takes to inspire someone else. So imagine if you did something heroic one **million** times.

Oh, and one last thing: Don't be afraid to fail. It happens. That's how you learn. I mean, me and Jake did everything we could to help dumb ol' Ice King find Gunter and he's still missing. We looked all over Ooo, but he didn't turn up once. Maybe he took off to become a hero on his own. Who knows? But tomorrow is a new day, and we'll never give up trying. That's what heroes do: **Never. Give. Up.**

YEAH! WHAT HE SAID!

TITAN
BOOKS

144 Southwark Street
London SE1 0UP
www.titanbooks.com

Find us on Facebook: www.facebook.com/titanbooks
Follow us on Twitter: @TitanBooks

Published by Titan Books, London, in 2017.

Published by arrangement with Insight Editions, PO Box 3088, San Rafael, CA 94912, USA. www.insighteditions.com

A CIP catalogue record for this title is available from the British Library.
ISBN: 9781785655890

Publisher: Raoul Goff
Acquisitions Manager: Robbie Schmidt
Art Director: Chrissy Kwasnik
Executive Editor: Vanessa Lopez
Production Editor: Elaine Ou
Editorial Assistant: Katie DeSandro
Production Managers: Blake Mitchum and Lina sp Temena
Production Assistant: Jacob Frink

REPLANTED PAPER

Insight Editions, in association with Roots of Peace, will plant two trees for each tree used in the
manufacturing of this book. Roots of Peace is an internationally renowned humanitarian organization
dedicated to eradicating land mines worldwide and converting war-torn lands into productive farms and
wildlife habitats. Roots of Peace will plant two million fruit and nut trees in Afghanistan and provide
farmers there with the skills and support necessary for sustainable land use.

Manufactured in China by Insight Editions

10 9 8 7 6 5 4 3 2 1

Gunter was in the closet all along! I didn't even think to look there because it's his favorite place. Now that I see that sentence on paper I feel like a real idiot.